EGMONT

We bring stories to life

This edition published in Great Britain 2011
by Dean, an imprint of Egmont UK Limited
239 Kensington High Street, London W8 6SA

CARTOON NETWORK, the logo, BEN 10 and all related characters and
elements are trademarks of and © 2011 Cartoon Network.

Adapted from the animated series by
Barry Hutchison

ISBN: 978 0 6035 6584 7

1 3 5 7 9 10 8 6 4 2

Printed and bound in Singapore

A CIP catalogue record for this title is available from
the British Library

BEN 10

FAVOURITE STORIES

CONTENTS

AND THEN THERE WERE 10

BEN TENNYSON IS A 10-YEAR-OLD KID WHO'S JUST FINISHED SCHOOL FOR THE SUMMER. HE'S OFF ON A ROAD TRIP WITH HIS GRANDPA MAX IN THEIR OLD 'RV' – THE RUSTBUCKET! MEANWHILE, STRANGE THINGS ARE HAPPENING IN OUTER SPACE . . . .

CHAPTER ONE

MEET BEN TENNYSON

*I*n outer space, a small alien spaceship spun to avoid the energy blasts of a battleship following it.

BLAM! The smaller ship has been hit! It fired back and burnt two deep holes in the side of the larger ship.

On board the battleship, a huge alien leaned forwards in his command chair. His name was Vilgax, and he was very angry!

'I have come too far to be denied!' he growled, clenching his fists. 'The Omnitrix shall be mine and no one will dare to stand in my way!'

7

Thousands of miles away, Ben Tennyson was in the school playground. School was over, and the holidays were just beginning!

He spotted two older kids pushing around a much smaller boy. The younger boy was Jamie from Ben's class.

'Normally, we'd take your money and beat you up, but since it's the last day of school we're gonna give you a break,' snarled one of the bullies. 'Now, hand over the cash!'

'Leave him alone!'

The bullies spun round to find Ben standing nearby. They laughed when they saw him. Not only were they bigger, but there was two of them and only one of him.

'Get lost, shrimp!'

'I said,' growled Ben, 'back off!'

 He clenched his fists. It was time to teach these bullies a lesson!

Instead, Ben found himself dangling from a tree branch by his underwear. Jamie hung helplessly beside him – another victim of the bullies' famous Atomic Wedgie!

'Thanks,' Jamie sighed. 'Thanks a lot!'

Shaking and spitting out black smoke, a tatty motor-home stopped just outside the school gates. A friendly-looking old man wound down the window and leaned out.

'Come on, Ben, let's go!' he shouted. 'I want to make it to the campsite by nightfall.'

Ben rolled his eyes. 'Uh, Grandpa,' he called, 'a little help here?'

Grandpa Max climbed back into the motor-home. The floor creaked as he made his way to the driver's seat. He didn't call the van The Rust Bucket for nothing!

Ben pushed the door closed behind him and followed Grandpa Max.

'I've been so looking forward to this,' he grinned.

Ben stopped in his tracks as he realised they were not alone. His cousin, Gwen, was also there.

'What are you doing here?' he asked. Ben spun back to face Grandpa Max. 'What is *she* doing here?'

'This wasn't my idea,' Gwen explained. 'My mom said that going camping for the summer would be good for me.'

'I can't believe it,' Ben moaned. 'I wait all year for this trip and now the Queen of Cooties is coming too!'

'Hey, I had my own vacation planned too, ya know,' replied Gwen. 'Now, I'm stuck with my geekazoid cousin for three months!'

Grandpa Max started The Rust Bucket's engine. 'Something tells me it's going to be a long summer,' he sighed.

CHAPTER TWO

GOING HERO

Ben and Gwen sat at a picnic table, surrounded by tall trees. They had arrived at the campsite just as it was getting dark.

'Chow time!' Grandpa Max announced. He stepped down from The Rust Bucket holding a large plate. Dinner smelled great! Ben hadn't realised how hungry he was until now.

But not that hungry. Ben stared down at the slimy mass on the plate set before them.

It looked disgusting, and it was moving!

'What *is* that?' Ben said, as half his dinner began to crawl across the table.

'Marinated mealworms,' announced Grandpa Max, proudly. 'And if these don't sound good, I've got some sheep's tongue.'

'Couldn't we just have a burger or something?'

'Nonsense!' laughed Grandpa Max. 'I'll grab the tongue.'

'OK,' whispered Ben to Gwen, 'I got half a bag of corn chips and a candy bar in my backpack. What you got?'

'Some rice cakes and hard candy.'

It wasn't much, but it was better than worms. 'Think they'll last the whole summer?'

The two ships were still locked in battle. Vilgax's second-in-command scanned the controls. 'Their propulsion systems have been destroyed,' it announced.

'Prepare to board,' barked Vilgax. 'I want the Omnitrix now!'

Suddenly, an energy blast exploded! Vilgax roared with rage.

He flipped open a panel on his chair and stabbed at the controls. He activated the ship's most powerful weapon as another explosion hit Vilgax's ship.

A bolt of energy shot from the front of Vilgax's ship. With a flash, half of the smaller ship was turned into specks of dust.

Unseen by Vilgax, a hatch slid open in the belly of the shattered ship. A small pod emerged and raced towards a distant planet. The planet Earth!

Meanwhile, Ben was in the forest near the campsite. He'd had enough of Gwen. Why did Grandpa have to bring her along? This was going to be the worst vacation ever.

Something overhead caught his eye. He looked up and saw a bright light streaking across the sky.

Ben watched the light. It seemed to be getting brighter and bigger. He suddenly realised that it was shooting straight for him!

Ben moved out of the way just as the ground where he'd been standing exploded with a **BOOM!**

The whole area was covered in dust. As it cleared, Ben edged forwards. The meteorite had left a large crater in the forest. He crept closer and saw a small metal ball at the bottom of the hole.

Suddenly the ground at Ben's feet crumbled. He slid into the crater and skidded to a stop next to the sphere. It opened, revealing an eerie green glow.

Ben leaned in closer. There was something inside the ball – something very un-alien.

'A watch?' he frowned. 'What's that doing in outer space?'

Without warning, the device leaped out of its protective shell. It wrapped round Ben's wrist and clamped on tight.

'Get it off! Get it off!' he shouted, trying to shake it off his arm. He pulled hard, but the watch was stuck!

Ben climbed out of the crater. He yanked at the watch, but it continued to cling on.

He studied it more closely. How was he supposed to tell the time? Instead of hands, it had some odd symbols, with three green rings round the outside.

As he fiddled with the device, it suddenly let out a loud **BLEEP!** The middle of the watch raised up and a figure shaped like a man appeared on the display.

'Cool!'

He pushed the raised part of the watch back down and a strange green energy swirled out then up his arm. As the energy passed across him, his body began to mutate. Ben closed his eyes. He was terrified!

When he opened his eyes, Ben was much bigger and covered in flames! He didn't know it yet, but he was now an alien called Heatblast.

'I'm on fire!' he cried, before realising the flames weren't hurting him.

He glanced at a nearby tree, then pointed to one of its branches. A blast of flame shot from his fingertip. 'Now that's what I'm talking about!'

He squeezed his hands together. A fire-ball shot from his hands, snapping a row of trees in half and igniting their leaves.

'Stop!' yelped Heatblast. But as the smouldering leaves hit the grass, the blaze quickly took hold. The forest was on fire!

CHAPTER THREE

A FLAMING DISASTER

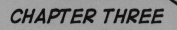

What's that?' asked Gwen, pointing towards a bright glow in the sky above some nearby trees.

'Looks like a forest fire,' Grandpa Max replied. 'We'd better let the ranger know. Probably some foolish camper messing around with something they shouldn't.'

Grandpa Max and Gwen stood in silence. A terrible thought came to them both.

'Ben!'

'Take this,' said Grandpa Max, throwing Gwen a fire extinguisher. Taking one for himself, they set off in the direction of the glow.

In the heart of the forest, Heatblast was trying to stamp out the fire. But every time his foot touched the ground, his flames set  something alight. The fire was out of control!

Suddenly, a blast of white foam hit him in the face. He spluttered, choking on the spray.

When he recovered, Heatblast found himself face to face with Gwen. Foam dripped from the nozzle of her fire extinguisher. She stared at the alien, then screamed loudly.

'I know I look weird,' Heatblast said, 'but there's no reason to be scared. . .'

But it wasn't Gwen who needed to be scared. Recovering from her fright, she swung the fire extinguisher. It made a loud clang as it hit Heatblast's head, sending him tumbling to the ground.

'I don't know what you are, but you'll stay down there if you know what's good for you,' she warned, holding up the extinguisher.

The alien's eyes narrowed. 'Don't even think about it, freak.'

Gwen stopped in her tracks. Only one person called her 'freak'.

'Ben?' she gasped.

Heatblast filled her in. He was getting to the part where he'd set the forest on fire when Grandpa Max came running up.

'Gwen, are you all . . .' he began, before spotting Heatblast. 'What in blazes?'

'It's me, Grandpa!'

'Ben?' frowned Grandpa Max. 'What happened to you?'

'Well, when I was walking, this meteor –'

'Um, excuse me,' Gwen interrupted, 'major forest fire burning out of control? What do we do?'

Grandpa Max thought for a few moments. 'Backfire,' he said at last. 'Start a new fire and let it burn into the old fire. They'll snuff each other out. Think you can do that, Ben?'

'Shooting flames I can definitely do!'

He ran towards the fire until he was in an untouched area of forest.

Concentrating, Heatblast threw out his hands. A surge of power shot along his arms, before a jet of flame leaped from his fingertips. It only took a few seconds for the new fire to take hold.

Within minutes, the two fires met and began to snuff each other out. Heatblast had saved the day! With a little help from Grandpa, of course.

Vilgax was hurt, but still alive. He had lost more than half his body when the deck had exploded from the energy blast. Now he floated in a Medi-Tube, breathing through the ship's life-support systems.

'This battle nearly cost me my life,' he wheezed, 'and you say the Omnitrix is no longer on board the transport?'

'Sensors indicate a probe was sent out from the ship,' his robot explained. 'It landed on a nearby planet.'

What was left of Vilgax's face twisted into a scowl. 'Go,' he ordered. 'Bring it to me!'

'And you say that this "watch" just jumped up and clamped on to your wrist?' asked Grandpa Max. They were sitting by the campfire, watching to make sure nothing else went up in smoke.

'Hey, it wasn't my fault,' Heatblast insisted.

'I believe you, Ben,' nodded Grandpa.

'Will he stay a monster forever?' asked Gwen. She hoped the answer would be 'yes.'

'He's an alien,' Grandpa Max replied. Gwen and Heatblast were staring at him quizzically.

'I mean look at him,' he added quickly. 'What else could he be?'

'But don't worry, Ben,' Grandpa Max quickly reassured him. 'We'll figure this thing out.'

They all jumped with fright as the watch gave a loud **BLEEP!** Heatblast stood up as a few more beeps rang out, then he was lit up by a flash.

Ben looked at himself. His hands were his own. His clothes were his own. Even better, he was no longer on fire!

'I'm me again!' cried Ben. 'But I still can't get this watch off.'

'Better not fool with it until we know what we're dealing with,' warned Grandpa Max. He stood up. 'I'll check out the crash site. You guys stay here.'

Gwen and Ben watched him disappear into the trees. Neither of them noticed the sleek shape that moved silently down from the sky above their heads.

CHAPTER FOUR

GIVE A DOG A DRONE

The robot stood at the edge of the crater, looking for the Omnitrix. It detected the metal shell, but realised it was empty. Someone had taken the watch!

Two hidden compartments in the robot's shoulders unfolded, allowing a pair of spinning discs to fly free. As they flew through the forest, a set of metal claws extended below them both.

If the Omnitrix was nearby, they'd find it. It was only a matter of time.

Ben sat with his back against The Rust Bucket, fiddling with the watch. He couldn't figure out what made the thing tick.

'Caught ya!' Gwen yelled.

'Very funny,' Ben snapped. 'Like your face.'

'Grandpa said not to mess with that thing,' she reminded him.

'Come on,' said Ben, 'aren't you a little bit curious about what it can do?'

'Not in the least.'

Ben looked Gwen up and down. 'Are you sure we're related?' He turned back to the watch. 'If I can figure this thing out, maybe I can help people. Not just make things worse.'

He twisted the watch. With a **BLEEP!** the centre raised up once more.

'Hey, I think I've figured out how I did it,' he said. 'Should I try it again, just once?'

'I wouldn't.'

'No, duh,' Ben mocked his cousin, 'you wouldn't.'

He slammed his hand down on the watch, and was swallowed up by the cloud of weird energy. But this time, there were no flames.

Instead, Ben felt thick, wiry hairs burst through his skin. Fangs tore up through his bottom jaw and claws sprouted from his fingers and toes. With a loud roar, Ben transformed into the savage Wildmutt!

'Eww!' Gwen winced. 'This thing's even uglier than you are normally.'

Wildmutt opened his mouth to reply, but all that came out were some strange groans.

'And no eyes?' scoffed Gwen. 'What good is this one? It can't see!'

A wicked thought occurred to her. Gwen picked up a stick and crept over to the huge, dog-like alien. She swung the stick, full speed, towards Wildmutt.

The blind alien's senses detected the threat, and it sprang into action. Gwen gasped as it backflipped out of danger and onto the roof of The Rust Bucket.

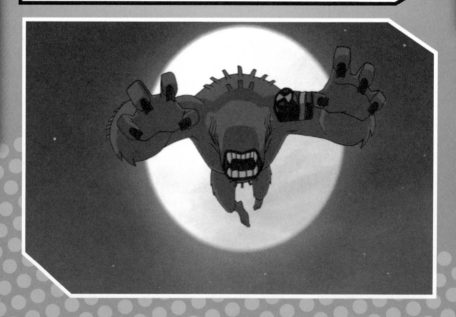

'OK, so maybe it's not a total loser,' Gwen admitted. The alien leaped down from the motor-home and landed in front of her. Wildmutt snorted, then turned away. He kicked his back legs, spraying Gwen with mud, then ran off into the trees.

'Ben, get back here! I'm gonna tell Grandpa that you turned into some freaky animal-monster thing and went into the forest when he told you not to.'

She replayed her entire last sentence in her head. 'This,' Gwen sighed, 'has been a majorly weird day.'

Wildmutt swung from branch to branch. Although he couldn't see, his other senses guided him.

As he landed on another branch, his fur stood on end. Something bad was about to happen!

A laser blast lit up the forest and turned the branch beneath Wildmutt to splinters. He leaped for another tree as one of the robot's deadly drones came spinning from the shadows.

The alien launched himself forwards as the tree he'd just swung from exploded. Faster – he had to move faster!

Another tree erupted into flames. The stench of burning filled his nostrils. Wildmutt could taste the smoke – thick and black. The perfect place to hide.

The drone began scanning for any sign of the beast. A sudden sound made it spin round. Wildmutt sailed through the air, landing on the flying disc!

He began to tear it apart; his teeth ripping into the drone's electrics. It zigzagged through the trees, trying to shake Wildmutt off. He clung on, as it shuddered. Time to get off this ride!

Wildmutt somersaulted to safety. The watch then started to bleep, and the alien transformation wore off. He was Ben again.

'Yesss!' he cheered. He'd won!

Then Ben heard a low humming sound. A second robot drone hovered in the treetops, its weapons trained on him.

'Oh,' Ben gulped. 'Not good.'

CHAPTER FIVE

DIAMOND GEEZER

*B*en tried to stumble away, but the drone hovered closer. It detected that he had the Omnitrix and switched its weapons to full power. One blast would destroy the human.

CLANG! A spade smashed into the drone. The impact short-circuited its flight systems and it crashed to the ground. A red-haired girl stood over it, looking down.

'Back off, sparky,' Gwen snarled. She raised her spade and hit down hard on the drone's robotic disc. It was destroyed!

When Ben and Gwen were safely back inside The Rust Bucket, Grandpa Max began his lecture.

'I asked you not to fool around with that thing until we know what it is.'

'Sorry, Grandpa,' Ben said. 'But at least I've figured it out. You press this button, then when the ring pops up, twist it until you see the guy you want to be. Slam it down and **BAMMO!** You're a super-cool alien dude!'

'What about not transforming back into plain old pizza-face?' Gwen scowled.

'I haven't figured that out yet,' admitted Ben.

With a loud crackle, The Rust Bucket's short-range radio switched on.

'Mayday! Mayday! Somebody help us!' pleaded a frightened voice. 'We're under attack by some sort of. . . robot!'

The rest of the transmission was drowned out by static.

'Sounds just like those things that attacked me,' Ben said. 'It must be looking for the watch. Those people are in trouble because of me.' He looked at Grandpa Max. 'I think I can help them.'

Ben threw open The Rust Bucket's door. Gwen and Grandpa Max followed him outside. Ben spun the outside ring of the watch.

'Eenie, meanie, minie . . .' He stopped at one of the alien outlines. 'Here it goes!'

BLEEP! went the watch. Ben's hand slammed down. A familiar cloud of energy swirled across his body.

'So what can this guy do?' Gwen demanded.

'I don't know.' Ben shrugged. 'But I bet it's gonna be cool!'

At a nearby campsite, Vilgax's robot was destroying everything in its path. Motor-homes and tents exploded as it unleashed its power blasts. It had extended to its full height, towering like a giant above the wreckage.

Campers ran, trying to get to safety. The robot wanted the Omnitrix, and it was going to find it, no matter what.

The android swung an arm down and grabbed one of the fleeing campers. The man screamed and kicked, struggling to break free of the robot's clutches.

'Leave him alone!' boomed a voice from close by.

A large alien, made of what looked like green crystal, appeared. It was Ben in the form of the indestructible Diamondhead.

'You want somebody to pick on?' he growled. 'Try me!'

The robot scanned the newcomer. It dropped the camper, as its targeting system locked onto the watch. It had found the Omnitrix!

A blast of energy screeched from its weapons and slammed into the ground at Diamondhead's feet.

The alien was thrown into the air and through the roof of a motor-home.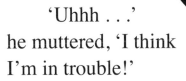

'Uhhh . . .' he muttered, 'I think I'm in trouble!'

A dazed Diamondhead pulled himself up and gave his head a shake. If he could just take a moment to recover, he'd –

No time! He threw himself clear, just before a power blast turned the motor-home into an oily spot on the ground.

Before Diamondhead could get back to his feet, the robot wrapped a huge, metal claw round him and lifted him into the air.

He felt a sharp pain shoot through his shoulder as the android gave a violent tug. Diamondhead gasped as he realised what was happening.

The robot was tearing him apart!

CHAPTER SIX

A TASTE OF THEIR OWN MEDICINE

Diamondhead gritted his teeth. If he didn't do something quick, his arm was going to be ripped off!

He forced shards of diamond to extend out from his trapped arm. They tore through the robot's metal claw, damaging the wiring inside. The android's arm exploded!

The robot then blasted Diamondhead, sending him hurtling towards a toilet block. The alien smashed through the brick walls.

'Ben!' shouted Grandpa Max helplessly. But Diamondhead wasn't done for yet. He threw up his arms as the android launched another blast.

He watched as the beams reflect of his shiny body. The polished surface acted like a mirror. It gave Diamondhead an idea.

'Come on!' he barked at his enemy.

The robot fired his weapon. With a roar, Diamondhead held up his hands and pushed back against the blast, deflecting its deadly beam.

The laser sliced the robot neatly in two. Twin explosions ripped through both broken parts, destroying them from the inside out.

Ben had defeated the robot!

MEANWHILE . . .

Inside his life-support tube, Vilgax was furious. He had been following events on his ship's viewing screen.

'Failure,' he scowled. 'Unbelievable! That puny Earth-being is keeping the Omnitrix from me!'

Soon he would make the boy pay. Soon he would make the whole pathetic planet pay!

Vilgax looked down at the stumps where his legs should be.

Soon, but not quite yet . . .

The next morning, Grandpa and Gwen were packing up The Rust Bucket.

Grandpa looked around. 'Where's Ben?'

Gwen shrugged. 'I haven't seen him.'

A sleek alien named XLR8 skidded to a halt beside a shocked Grandpa Max.

'Ben?'

'Yup,' the alien replied. 'Check this out!'

They'd hardly noticed the alien move, but all their belongings were now neatly stacked inside The Rust Bucket.

'Pretty fast, huh?' beamed XLR8.

With a **BLEEP BLEEP BLEEEEP!** the alien turned back into Ben Tennyson.

'It's going to be the best summer ever,' he grinned.

'It's definitely going to be interesting,' Gwen agreed. 'So, where'd you go, anyway?'

'Just had to take care of a few things,' he smirked.

Back in the playground of Ben's school, two bullies found themselves dangling from a tree by their underwear. How had they got there? Neither one of them knew. Whatever had happened to them had happened very, very fast!

Ben couldn't help but chuckle as he sat in The Rust Bucket. That robot wasn't the only one to have been given a taste of its own medicine!

Ben wasn't sure what lay ahead, but he knew it was going to be a lot of fun finding out!

TOURIST TRAP

AFTER DEFEATING VILGAX'S ROBOT
DRONES, BEN, GWEN AND GRANDPA
MAX ARE BACK ON THEIR ROAD TRIP IN
THE RUST BUCKET. BUT IT'S NOT LONG
BEFORE A TRAFFIC JAM BECOMES
DANGEROUS AND THEY HAVE TO TURN
TO A SLIMY ALIEN HERO FOR HELP . . .

CHAPTER ONE

A FIRE FLY SQUEEEAK!

Ben dragged his nose across the window of The Rust Bucket, leaving a trail of snot. He puffed out his cheeks, pressed his lips to the glass and crossed his eyes. He looked like the world's ugliest fish.

In the next lane of the busy motorway, a boy in another car looked on, laughing. He and Ben were locked in battle. The boy hooked his fingers in the corners of his mouth and pulled, waggling his tongue.

It was a scary-face duel, and they were evenly matched.

Gwen looked at her cousin and sighed.

'I'd warn you that you face might freeze like that,' she said, 'but it would be an improvement.'

In the other car, his opponent now opened up his mouth. A soggy mush of chewed-up cheeseburger was on the end of his tongue.

'Oh, man! The "see-food special"!' Ben groaned. There was only one way he could win the duel now.

Hiding out of sight, he hit the centre of the Omnitrix. 'Time for my secret weapon.'

A wad of green goo hit the inside of The Rust Bucket's window. A hideous, insect-like face appeared, ooze dripping from its antennae. Ben had transformed into the alien, Stinkfly!

The boy screamed in terror. In the front of their car, his dad turned round to see what was going on. He saw Stinkfly and screamed too!

The alien watched as their car sped away then collapsed on the floor, giggling. Gwen shook her head in disgust.

'There is such a thing as taking a joke too far,' she scowled. She went to sit down then cried out in shock as she sat in a pile of alien slime!

Stinkfly erupted into more laughter. 'Impossible!' he cried. 'Funny is funny!'

'Ben, get up here!' Grandpa Max's voice sounded serious. Something had to be wrong.

With a screech of brakes, The Rust Bucket came to a sudden stop.

'We got trouble ahead,' said Grandpa.

Grandpa Max, Gwen and Stinkfly stared at the tangle of metal blocking the road ahead. A truck had crashed into a fuel tanker, and flames surrounded both vehicles.

Inside the truck's cab, they could just make out the shape of the the driver. He was hammering against the doors but they were jammed shut. The driver was trapped!

'If the fuel catches fire that truck will become a rocket to the moon,' said Grandpa.

Stinkfly didn't hesitate. He kicked open the door of The Rust Bucket and launched himself towards the flaming wreckage. Grandpa Max and Gwen made sure the crowd of onlookers stayed out of danger.

The heat from the fire was blistering. Even with all his alien power, Stinkfly struggled to get close enough to the driver.

'The fire's too intense. I wish I was Heatblast,' he muttered. A thought suddenly occurred to him. 'Hey, that gives me an idea.'

Stinkfly's wings buzzed, carrying him above the flames and closer to the truck. Clouds of black smoke swirled around him, making it hard to see. He would only have one chance at this, so it had to work.

SPU-LAT!

A thick ball of goo spat from one of Stinkfly's antennae. It splattered on to a burning chunk of metal. The slime smothered the flames, snuffing them out.

SPU-LAT!
SPU-LAT!
SPU-LAT!

More dollops rained down, coating the wreckage and the ground in a layer of goo. Inside the truck, the driver was terrified. One minute he could see a raging fire, the next the windows were covered in sludge. He had no idea what was going on.

Suddenly a pair of claws ripped through the roof of the cab. Four insect-like arms picked up the driver and carried him off into the air. It was Stinkfly!

'Loogies save lives,' he said, placing the driver safely back down on the ground.

'Aaah!' screamed a crowd of onlookers. The boy from the car was pointing at him.

Grandpa Max looked at Stinkfly, who swallowed nervously. He wouldn't be happy that Ben had used the Omnitrix to win a face-pulling contest.

'Gotta fly!' Stinkfly said, buzzing off.

Ben was back in The Rust Bucket. Grandpa Max was driving to their next stop. It was going to be a surprise.

Gwen spotted a road sign.

'You'll have a ball with It,' she read. 'Next exit.'

'Come on, Grandpa,' Ben pleaded. 'Give us a hint of what It is.'

Grandpa Max shook his head. 'No hints.' He drove off the motorway then guided the motor-home to a stop by the roadside.

'Now,' said Grandpa Max, 'both of you close your eyes.'

Grandpa Max jumped out of The Rust Bucket. He took both children by the hand and led them out of the motor-home.

'OK, open them up,' he grinned.

Ben and Gwen opened their eyes. Before them stood a street full of run-down buildings.

On top of many of the buildings were giant novelty props. A ten-metre-long hot dog sat on one roof. A huge glass bowl on another.

Lame didn't even begin to describe the place, thought Ben.

'Ta-da!' cried Grandpa, grinning. He pointed up to a big sign:

'Welcome to Sparksville!'

CHAPTER TWO

IT

*G*randpa Max bounced up and down.

'Is this place great or what?'

Ben looked around. 'Uh . . . I'll go with "or what".'

'Come on, what's more exciting than the world's biggest fish bowl?'

Ben thought about this for a second. 'Everything?'

A tall skinny man wearing a suit shuffled over to join the group.

'As the Mayor of Sparksville, I welcome you to our town, O, seekers of wonder,' he drawled, before shuffling back the way he came.

Grandpa turned to his grandchildren. 'I know you are excited to see It,' he said. 'so I'll go check us in.'

Grandpa gave Ben two tickets for the exhibition then went off to the motel. Ben and Gwen walked towards the sign: 'Exciting Exhibits'.

They arrived at a ticket booth. A doorway led to an area surrounded by a tall fence. Like the rest of Sparksville, the booth seemed to be deserted.

DING! Ben rang the bell on the desk. A familiar figure stepped through the doorway.

'Tickets, please,' droned the man.

'I thought you were the mayor?' said Ben with a frown.

The mayor shrugged before taking their tickets. With Gwen following, Ben went into the exhibition area.

The exhibits were even less impressive than Ben and Gwen had expected. There was a robotic jackalope: a mythical creature with the body of a rabbit and the horns of an antelope. The one on display had a set of antlers missing. Its mouth made a mechanical whir as it chomped on a large cardboard carrot.

There was The World's Biggest House Of Cards, which they had imagined to be a carefully arranged stack of thousands of playing cards in the shape of a house. Instead there were seven extremely large playing cards, stacked up to make a sort of triangle shape that wobbled as they walked past.

The world's biggest fish bowl was just a really large – and completely empty – glass bowl. The enormous hot dog they had seen from outside was nothing more than a billboard for a snack shop.

They continued on until they arrived at an old barn. Painted on the outside in metre-high letters were two short words words: IT'S HERE.

CREEEEAK!

The doors to the barn swung open, revealing nothing but darkness.

'Please tell me this is It,' Ben sighed. 'Because I can't stand It any more.'

As they walked through, several signs began to illuminate on the walls.

'Do not touch It,' Ben read.

'Do not photograph It,' said Gwen.

'Do not use batteries or electrical equipment anywhere near It,' Ben continued.

He had to admit, whatever It was, it was starting to sound almost interesting.

But a second later, Ben realised he could not have been more wrong...

'This is It?' he snorted, as they arrived at a wide, looming object.

'It's a big ball of rubber bands,' said Gwen.

The mayor suddenly appeared. 'But who knows what secrets lie within?'

'More rubber bands?' suggested Ben.

'Stay as long as you like,' the mayor told them. 'Mind the signs.'

Ben waited for him to leave before turning to Gwen. 'Look at this place!' he complained. 'We've been punked.'

'It is pretty lame,' Gwen admitted.

She spotted a mischievous expression on Ben's face. 'I know that look,' she said. 'What are you planning?'

Ben slammed his hand down on the Omnitrix. A swirl of green energy surrounded him. He transformed into the powerful alien, Four Arms.

Four Arms scooped up the rubber band ball and began bouncing it up and down. 'One good prank deserves another,' he said.

Gwen smirked. 'For once, I agree with you. Got something special in mind?'

He flicked the ball into the air and balanced it on his shoulders. It wobbled back and forth.

'Careful, dweeb. You'll drop it,' Gwen warned.

'Not a chance,' Four Arms replied. He caught the ball with one hand and held it above his head. 'I could lift this thing with three arms tied behind my –'

The ball rolled off the alien's hand. It boinged on the floor then shot upwards, smashing through the roof with a **KER-ASH!**

Four Arms looked up at the roof and winced. 'Oops.'

Outside the ball bounced off on a path of destruction. It crashed down on the gift shop, then smashed the giant hot dog to pieces. Several other exhibits were destroyed before the ball came to a halt among the ruins of the house of cards.

Four Arms and Gwen rushed over to check out the damage. Things were pretty bad. Half of the exhibits were broken.

As Four Arms began to pick up the fallen cards, Gwen slapped him hard across the back of the head.

'Ow! What was that for?' he demanded.

'That's for turning me into a criminal,' Gwen snapped.

The alien smiled. 'Don't get your shorts in a twist. I'll just put everything back the way it was.'

As he gripped the ball, the Omnitrix gave a sudden bleep.

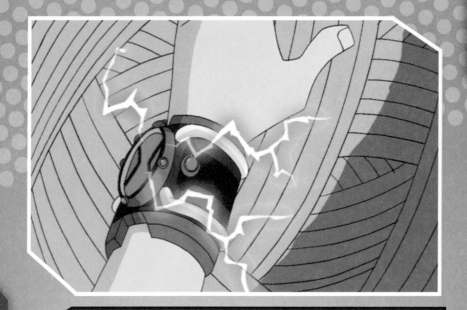

In a flash of light, Four Arms changed back into Ben.

'OK,' Ben gulped. 'Maybe a little problem.'

The cousins were so busy worrying about what to do that neither one noticed the sparks of red energy crackling across the surface of the Omnitrix. They flashed like tiny bolts of lightning, before being drawn into the rubber band ball.

At that very moment, deep inside the ball, something began to stir . . .

CHAPTER THREE

WHAT'S A MEGAWHATT?

*G*randpa Max had checked them into the Sideways Motel. Like everywhere in Sparksville, the motel had a theme, and the clue to this particular theme was in the title.

Ben and Gwen stared at the door to their room. It was sideways on the wall, so they would have to crawl on the floor to get through the door.

'What are we going to tell Grandpa?' Gwen fretted.

'Nothing,' replied Ben. 'We just play dumb.'

'Easy for you. You're a lot better at it than I am.' She opened the door and crawled inside.

'Hey, there you are!' cried Grandpa Max, as Gwen and Ben clambered through.

The inside of the room was very odd. The whole room looked like it had been tipped on its side. One of the walls was completely covered in carpet with tables and chairs attached. Even the beds were stuck to the wall.

Grandpa Max stood in the middle of the room. The floor beneath his feet was covered in wallpaper.

'Isn't this place a riot?' Grandpa Max grinned.

OVER AT THE HOUSE OF CARDS . . .

The rubber band ball was beginning to shudder and shake. Electrical energy flew out of the rubber and snaked through the air until it found overhead power cables.

Energy crackled and fizzed. Large sparks shot off in all directions. One spark burned a hole through the town's welcome sign.

POP!

A small black-and-yellow shape squeezed out of the rubber ball. Energy buzzed behind his eyes, as the creature laughed manically.

He had been imprisoned for too long, but now his powers had returned. He was free.

Sunlight streamed in through the window of the sideways bedroom. Ben and Gwen slowly woke up. It had been a long night. After taking nearly an hour to get into their beds, they had slept tangled up in their bed covers like hammocks.

'What the heck happened?' Grandpa's voice jolted the cousins awake. They both slipped from their beds and hit the floor with a bump.

'Argh! He knows everything!' said Gwen in a panicked whisper. 'We have to come clean.'

Ben shook his head. 'Sometimes it's hard to believe you're really a kid. Never admit anything until you absolutely have to.'

'Benjamin. Gwendolyn. Get out here,' Grandpa Max barked.

'"Gwendolyn"?' gulped Gwen. 'We're doomed.'

They got dressed and hurried outside.

Grandpa Max was on the main street. Every exhibit, stand and shop front was smashed or smoking. It was much worse than the damage Four Arms had caused.

'What happened?' asked Ben.

'I don't know,' said Grandpa Max. 'Looks like a tornado tore through.'

Ben smiled. They were off the hook. 'Good,' he said. 'I mean, yeah. It was just one of those freaky nature things.'

The mayor stepped up to join them.

'It's pretty clear who's responsible for these juvenile acts,' he droned.

'"Juvenile acts"?' repeated Grandpa Max. He turned to Ben and Gwen. 'If I didn't know better, that sounds like –'

'Oh, I'm not talkin' about these youngsters,' interrupted the mayor.

Ben, Gwen and Grandpa all raised their eyebrows in surprise. "You're not?" they asked.

Suddenly, a bolt of electrical energy whizzed past Grandpa Max's ear. He turned to find a small black-and-yellow creature had sat on his shoulder, smiling at him.

The creature zapped away. It kicked Ben in the shins before leaping on to Gwen's back. She tried to shake it off, but it yanked the back of her T-shirt over her head.

'What . . . was that?' gasped Ben.

'Megawhatt,' drawled the mayor.

'Mega what?'

'Exactly.' The mayor nodded. 'Normally wrapped up tight inside of It. Until last night.'

Ben and Gwen exchanged a guilty glance, but said nothing.

'Some say it might be a ball of lightning come alive,' the mayor continued. 'Others think it's static cling run amok.'

'Maybe it's an alien,' suggested Gwen.

The mayor rolled his eyes. 'Alien? That's just plain kooky talk.'

They watched the creature climb inside a drinks vending machine. Electrical energy began to fizz across the machine's surface.

'What's it doing?' asked Ben.

'It eats electricity. The more it gobbles, the more powerful it gets.'

PTCHOOW!

A soft-drink can exploded from the machine's dispenser then rocketed towards them. Soon cans were hurtling through the air like cannonballs.

'It's also got a dangerous sense of humour,' the mayor continued as they all ran for cover.

'You left that inside a rubber-band ball all this time?' asked Grandpa Max. 'Wasn't that dangerous?'

'Not so long as people minded the signs,' sighed the mayor.

Ben bit his lip. 'All right, we did it! We're guilty!' he cried.

'So much for admit nothing,' muttered Gwen.

Grandpa Max glared at both of them. 'We'll talk about this later,' he said. 'But for now, how do we stop this thing, Mr Mayor?'

The mayor shrugged. 'Whatcha mean "we"?' he said. 'You let it out. You catch it.'

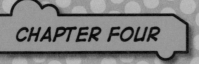

CHAPTER FOUR

THE APPLIANCE OF SCIENCE

Ben, Gwen and Grandpa walked along the near-deserted main street, looking for the Megawhatt. But so far the mischievous creature was staying hidden.

'Should we try to lure it out with some batteries or something?' asked Gwen.

Grandpa Max opened his mouth to reply, but a surge of electricity had shot up his trouser leg. He yelped with shock as the Megawhatt grabbed his underwear, lifting him off the ground. He hung in mid-air, caught in an atomic wedgie.

'That's not funny,' he groaned. 'It's just painful.'

'Don't worry, Grandpa,' said Ben, twisting the dial of the Omnitrix. 'I know just the hero to deal with this troublemaker!'

SLAM!

Ben's hand slapped down on the watch and energy wrapped around him. The shape-shifting Upgrade stood in Ben's place.

'Why go Upgrade?' asked Gwen.

'It's complicated. You wouldn't understand,' said the alien.

Gwen smirked. 'The watch didn't let you change into what you wanted to, did it?'

'Shut up,' he muttered.

The Megawhatt had dropped Grandpa and was zipping off to cause more mayhem.

'OK, twinkle toes, time to go home!'

The Megawhatt looked down to see the rubber band ball rolling – Upgrade was running on top, moving it forwards!

TWANG!

As the ball rolled over debris, one of the bands snapped. It pinged through the air at supersonic speed and punched a hole in a car windscreen.

More bands sprung free. People threw themselves to the ground to avoid being hit.

'Whose side are you on?' cried Gwen.

Upgrade jumped down from the rubber band ball, scared of doing more damage. The Megawhatt floated out of reach, laughing loudly. It was delighted by the extra destruction.

Upgrade scowled angrily. As he did, a beam of energy flew from his single eye towards the Megawhatt, who just avoided being zapped.

'Whoa, that's new!' Upgrade gasped. He pointed up at the floating Megawhatt. 'Not so funny now, is it?'

The Megawhatt disagreed. Giggling, he twisted and weaved around the alien hero, ducking out of reach whenever Upgrade got too close.

With a desperate leap, Upgrade's hands wrapped round the Megawhatt. He held the creature until a blast forced him to let go.

'OK,' Upgrade groaned, his body shaking. 'Do not touch the electrical guy when you're made of metal.'

Nearby, Grandpa and Gwen were worried.

'How are we going to ground that devil?' Grandpa Max wondered.

'Grandpa, you're a genius!' cried Gwen.

THE BATTLE GOES ON . . .

Upgrade darted past, chased by mini lightning bolts. One hit him hard on the behind.

'That's it,' he growled. 'I'm pulling the plug on this guy's pranks.'

Upgrade tore a manhole cover from the ground and launched it like a discus. It hurtled through the air then sliced the Megawhatt in half.

The two halves hung suspended in the air. But to Upgrade's horror, they then became two Megawhatts!

Before Upgrade could do anything, the Omnitrix began to flash. With a beep, the alien turned back into human form.

Lightning struck the ground on either side of Ben. He ran, searching for a place to hide.

A truck came roaring towards him. It stopped suddenly and the passenger door swung open. Ben jumped in, closing the door.

It was Grandpa Max and Gwen in The Rust Bucket!

'What are you doing?' panted Ben.

Grandpa Max pointed out of the back window. A giant thermometer – a Sparksville exhibit – was on the back of the truck.

'Giving these sparklers a science lesson they won't forget,' Grandpa Max said with a grin.

The Megawhatts were behind the truck. Next to Grandpa Max, Gwen yanked a control lever.

'Hey, Mega-weirds,' she cried, 'come get us!'

The back of the truck lifted up. The thermometer slid off and stuck into the ground.

The Megawhatts were moving too fast to stop. They smacked into the thermometer, then vanished inside. The three heroes leaped out of the truck.

'What happened?' asked Ben.

'Just used the thermometer as a lightning rod,' said Gwen proudly. 'Who needs an alien superhero when you've got good old-fashioned brain power?'

They heard a cough. It was the mayor.

'Course,' he began, 'the ground is just one big conductor.'

Ben frowned. 'What does that mean?'

Gwen's jaw dropped open as she realised what she had done.

'It means the Megawhatts are zipping around underground until they find some way to get back to the surface.'

BRRRRRRING BRRRRRRRING!

The phone in a nearby payphone booth began to ring. A second later, more joined the chorus. In no time at all it sounded as though every phone in the town was ringing at once.

'They're in the underground phone lines,' Grandpa muttered, as sparks began to emerge from the telephones' handsets.

Ben and Gwen gasped as hundreds upon hundreds of tiny Megawhatts began spewing out from the telephones and crackled across the sky.

CHAPTER FIVE

PRANKED

Gwen watched, as the Megawhatts set about destroying the rest of Sparksville.

'Ben Tennyson, don't say a word,' she sighed.

'I'm just glad I wasn't the one who screwed up this time,' Ben said with a grin.

A swarm of creatures swooped past and settled on the giant hotdog display. They chomped through it hungrily, then patted their swollen bellies.

BUUUUUUURP!

The belch was so loud it shattered all the windows on the street. On top of a nearby building, a glass display case exploded.

Gwen spun to face her cousin. 'Don't just stand there, doofus. Dial up help!'

Ben held up the Omnitrix. The display was still red: it hadn't yet recharged. 'Duh! Like I haven't been trying.' He glanced along the street. 'Ah . . . where'd they go?'

'I don't know,' said Grandpa Max. 'But I don't think it's good.'

KA-BOOM!

The ground beneath them shook. A planetarium building crumbled and a towering robotic monster appeared. Its head, hands and feet were made up of models of the planets of the solar system. The rest of its enormous frame was made up of chunks of machinery.

It clanked towards the main highway with sparks of energy spitting from its joints.

'Come on,' said Grandpa Max, running to The Rust Bucket, 'we'll head it off in –'

He stopped and stared. His beloved motor-home was a mess: every one of its wheels had been removed and it was covered in bright green graffiti.

' "U am lame",' read Ben. 'That's weak.'

'Don't get me started on the grammar and the spelling,' Gwen said, scowling.

'I reckon they'll head for the big hydroelectric dam to power up,' droned the mayor. 'Then they'll just wipe out the next town and so on.'

A short distance away, sunlight shone off the only glass object not to have been shattered by the Megawhatts' belch. Ben and Gwen both looked at it and smiled.

'You thinking what I'm thinking?' asked Gwen.

'Yeah,' said Ben as the Omnitrix flicked back to green. 'Beat those pranksters at their own game.'

The planetarium robot hit its fists against the thick walls of the dam. Cracks began to appear in the rock, becoming wider with each punch.

WHOOOSH!

Suddenly flames engulfed the mechanoid, pushing it away from the dam wall. The alien hero, Heatblast, stood on the top of the dam, smiling down.

'This is your only warning,' Heatblast yelled. 'Knock off the funny business!'

Swinging wildly, the robot smashed against the dam, shaking it. Heatblast slipped and began tumbling towards the ground.

As he fell, Heatblast produced a blast of heat beneath his feet. He rode the flame trail down, banking at the last minute to avoid crashing on to the floor of the dam.

Soaring upwards, Heatblast reached the top of the dam as the robot clambered towards the dam's energy store. Heatblast had to stop it before the robot could reach the machinery or it would be too powerful to contain.

Turning sharply, the alien tried to close in on the robot, but couldn't slow down enough to make the turn. Heatblast struck the top of the dam before bouncing to a stop in the robot's path.

A planet-Mars-shaped foot caught the alien under the jaw. Heatblast was flipped backwards and smashed hard against a solid brick wall.

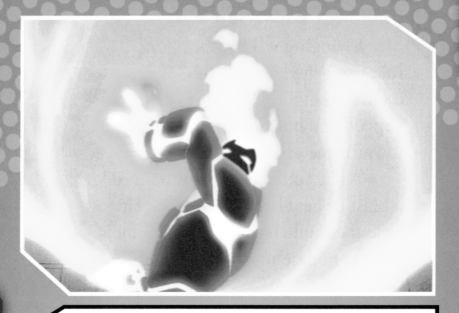

The robot advanced on the alien. But before meeting its target, Gwen stepped in front. She was holding the end of a hose.

'You guys are all wet,' she smirked, giving the nozzle a twist. A spray of water hit the robot in the face. It staggered away, thrashing its arms.

'What's the matter?' growled Heatblast, a huge fireball forming between his hands. 'Can't take a joke?' The ball of fire exploded around the robot, melting it into silver liquid.

The Megawhatts weren't laughing as they swarmed from the wreckage of their creation. As they flew angrily towards Heatblast, a cloud of black smoke suddenly sprang up and the Megawhatts began to cough and splutter. Their enemy was nowhere to be found.

'Missed me, doofus!' cried a voice above them.

The Megawhatts floated up to find Heatblast on the roof of the dam's control room. A large object stood behind him, covered by an even larger sheet.

Heatblast ducked beneath the sheet. The Megawhatts dived after him, passing through the fabric.

From behind the object, Grandpa Max cheered. 'Ben did it! They took the bait!'

He pulled away the sheet to reveal the world's largest fish bowl. Inside, the Megawhatts were trapped. With a blast of flame, Heatblast sealed the top, turning the bowl into a sphere of thick glass.

'Nice touch using the fish bowl,' Grandpa Max said. 'With non-conductive glass sealed up tight, they won't be going anywhere.'

'Science saves the day,' said Gwen.

The Omnitrix gave a bleep. Ben was himself once again.

'With a little help from science fiction,' he added.

As Ben, Gwen and Grandpa prepared to leave, they met the mayor. He was next to a new exhibit that had not yet been unveiled.

'I hope this wasn't a big setback for Sparksville,' Grandpa Max replied.

'More like a giant step forward, with our new attraction.' He pulled away the sheet covering the exhibit. The world's largest fish bowl was now the world's largest light bulb.

'It'll be a humdinger,' the mayor said. 'So long as folks mind the signs.'

There was a warning sign on the base of the light bulb. 'In case of emergency,' Ben read. 'Do not break the glass.'

KEVIN 11

BEN, GWEN AND GRANDPA MAX ARE ALL LOOKING FORWARD TO THE RUST BUCKET'S NEXT STOP – NEW YORK CITY. BUT BEN'S LOVE OF ARCADE GAMES CAUSES A BIG FAMILY ROW, LEADING HIM INTO A VERY DANGEROUS SITUATION...

CHAPTER ONE

THE BIG APPLE

The skyscrapers of New York City stretched above Ben, Grandpa and Gwen as they entered a large hotel. Instead of The Rust Bucket, they were going to be staying in a luxurious hotel!

While Grandpa Max checked in, Gwen looked through the building's brochure. With every word she read, she became more and more excited

'Wow, this hotel has everything!' she said. 'Indoor pool, spa . . .'

'Now, don't get used to it,' warned Grandpa Max. 'It's only for one night.'

As they walked towards the elevator to go up to their rooms, Ben stopped.

'Whoa!' he cried, spotting a sign above a door. It showed a character from Sumo Slammers, Ben's favourite TV show.

Ben ran over. Their latest video game wasn't out for ages, but a preview was taking place in that room. He had to get in!

A large security guard stopped him.

'Pass?' he growled.

'Must've left it inside,' Ben smiled. 'I'm one of the game pros testing out the system.'

Ben smiled confidently. The guard would definitely fall for that one.

'VIPs only.'

The guard hadn't fallen for it. Ben turned and slunk back to Grandpa Max and Gwen with his head hung low.

'I know what you're thinking,' Grandpa Max whispered. 'No sneaking back in there.'

'I won't,' Ben sighed. He watched as Grandpa Max and Gwen dragged their bags to the elevator. He wouldn't sneak in, but he knew an alien who would!

Making sure no one was watching, he activated the Omnitrix. A cloud of energy swirled over Ben, transforming him into Ghostfreak!

Making himself invisible, Ghostfreak floated past the security guard and through the closed doors.

It was Sumo Slammers heaven! Posters and cardboard cut-outs of the characters lined the walls.

Ghostfreak floated over to a games console and picked up a controller to play.

'The ultimate sneak peek,' he whispered, 'for the ghost with the most freak!'

But in the excitement of playing, Ben hadn't noticed the transformation wearing off. Over his shoulder, a large shape stepped forwards.

'What've you got to say for yourself, kid?' snarled the security guard.

Ben looked down at the Omnitrix and gasped. He was no longer Ghostfreak or invisible. 'Ah . . . "game over"?'

Outside the hotel, Grandpa Max's suitcase hit the pavement with a thud.

'And never come back!' warned the security guard, before stomping back to the hotel.

Grandpa Max, Ben and Gwen picked up their cases and climbed into The Rust Bucket.

'I told you not to sneak in there!' said Grandpa Max.

'Well, if you want to get all "technical" about it!' sulked Ben.

'How do you expect me to trust you if you keep misusing the watch?' Grandpa Max asked.

'I've used it a hundred times for good,' protested Ben. 'Why can't I use it just once for me?'

'It's not how many times you use it, Ben, it's how.'

Ben shrugged. 'It was no big deal.'

'To you. And that's all you care about,' glowered Grandpa Max. 'No more Sumo Slammers for two weeks.'

'No fair!' cried Ben.

'Neither's getting booted from a four-star hotel I already paid for!'

'Fine. Take it out of my allowance!'

'You don't get an allowance,' Gwen reminded him.

'Stay out of this!' snapped Ben and Grandpa Max together.

Ben scowled. 'You can't always tell me what to do. You're not my dad.'

'Well if I were...' began Grandpa Max.

But arguing was getting them nowhere. 'I'm going back to the hotel to see if I can get some of my money back,' he said. 'I won't be long.'

'Don't hurry,' muttered Ben. He stormed to the back of The Rust Bucket as Grandpa headed to the hotel.

'Totally not fair!' moaned Ben

'Glad to hear you're handling things so maturely,' said Gwen.

Ben pushed past her and jumped out of The Rust Bucket. 'Where are you going?' she demanded.

'Where does it look like? Out.'

Ben marched off along the street. Gwen hopped down after him. 'Get back here!'

'I don't speak dweeb.' Ben snapped.

Gwen watched him walk away, then decided to follow. 'You,' she sighed, 'are so grounded!'

A little way down the street, Ben found himself outside a video arcade. This would be the perfect place to chill out.

Gwen paused outside, listening to the bleeping of hundreds of video games.

'Next summer,' she sighed, 'I'm going to sleep-away camp.'

CHAPTER TWO

A NEW FRIEND?

Ben wandered through the arcade with eyes as wide as saucers. Every type of games machine was in this place. The only problem was deciding which one to play first.

He settled on a baseball simulator. Ben stepped on to the sensor plate, picked up the bat and dropped his coins into the slot. On the screen, an animated pitcher stepped up, ready to throw the ball.

Ben tightened his grip on the bat as he prepared to swing. As the pitcher wound up his arm to throw, the picture froze. The words 'Game Over' flashed up on the screen.

'Game over?' frowned Ben.

'It just started.' He spotted an attendant. 'This thing just ate all my tokens!' Ben complained.

'Read the sign, kid,' shrugged the attendant. 'It says "Play at your own risk".'

'This place is a rip off! Know that?!'

Over by another machine, a boy with long hair watched with interest.

'You're right,' the other boy said. 'The games here stink.'

'Yeah, but not as bad as his breath,' said Ben. 'Major case of sewer mouth.'

The boy laughed. 'You're funny,' he smiled. 'Here. You owe me one.'

He rested a hand on one of the machines. A wave of blue energy crackled from his fingertips. Almost at once, hundreds of tokens poured out from inside the cabinet.

'Whoa! How'd you do that?'

'I've got some skills.'

Ben scooped up the tokens. There were enough to keep him playing for months!

'We can't take those,' said Gwen, suddenly appearing behind him. 'They're not ours.'

'They are now,' Ben replied. 'Thanks,' he said to the boy. 'I'm Ben.'

'Kevin.'

'Wanna play some air hockey?'

Kevin started to say 'yes,' then stopped. Four teenagers were pushing through the crowds in his direction.

'Nuh. Gotta bail,' Kevin said. He turned and walked away quickly.

'He's total trouble,' Gwen warned.

'He seemed OK to me,' replied Ben. He watched as the gang members closed in on Kevin. His new friend was in trouble!

'Long time no see,' snarled one thug as he stepped in front of Kevin.

Kevin backed away, but two other gang members held him in place. He was trapped!

'Need some help?' asked Ben.

'Huh,' scoffed the leader. 'He's going to need a lot more than you. Beat it.'

He pushed Ben, sending him tumbling to the ground.

Ben leaped back to his feet. 'I've got some skills too,' he muttered. Ducking behind an arcade cabinet, he twisted the Omnitrix's dials. To take care of these thugs quickly, there was one alien he could always rely on.

'How's the hangout?' Kevin sneered at the gang leader. 'Still trashed like I left it for you?'

'You're gonna pay! You can't take us all alone, freak!'

'But I can!'

102

A strange figure stepped from behind a machine. Ben had transformed into the ultra-fast XLR8!

'Little early for Halloween, isn't it?' cackled one of the thugs.

XLR8 shot towards the group. He circled them, running faster and faster, until the gang leader was lifted off the ground. He screamed as he spun round and round.

Suddenly, XLR8 stopped. The gang leader hung in the air, then dropped back towards the floor. XLR8 flicked out his tail, slamming the thug against a wall.

XLR8 then shot off around the arcade. 'Where'd he go?' cried one of the gang.

A streak of speed lifted him up and crunched him down on top of the gang's boss. Soon all five gang members were stacked up against a wall.

XLR8 screeched to a halt next to Kevin. He saluted, then rocketed away before the transformation wore off.

A few minutes later, Gwen joined Ben outside the arcade. She scowled at him.'I can't believe you went alien!'

'He helped me, so I helped him. You wouldn't get it. Or Grandpa.' Ben snapped. 'That's the problem.'

'You see what that guy did to those losers?' cried Kevin, leaving the arcade.

'Yeah,' Ben smiled. 'Dude's name is XLR8. We're pretty tight.'

'Cool! Hey, want a tour of New York?'

'You keep Grandpa waiting any longer he's going to pop another gasket. We gotta go.' Gwen insisted.

Ben snorted. 'Don't you mean you have to go?'

'You're on your own,' Gwen sighed, walking off.

'Good. That's the way I want it.'

Ben turned his back on his cousin and followed Kevin through the back streets of New York City.

'So how'd you get your power?' Ben asked after a while.

'I was born with it,' Kevin explained. 'I'm like an energy sponge. Motors, lights, whatever. Soak it up, then dish it out when I want to.'

'Cool!'

'Come on,' said Kevin. 'I'll show you where I live.'

He led Ben through the streets until they reached an old abandoned subway station.

'You live here?' asked Ben.

'Yeah, by myself.'

'Where's your family?'

'Long gone.' Kevin shrugged. 'They weren't too thrilled at having a freak for a son. But it means I don't answer to nobody.'

'Sounds good to me. So why was that gang after you?'

'I trashed their hangout under the Thirty-Ninth Street bridge,' explained Kevin. 'What about you? Sounds like your grandpa's pretty steamed at you.'

Ben sighed. 'All I did was sneak in and play the new Sumo Slammers game.'

'The one that isn't out 'til Christmas?' Kevin asked.

'Yeah.'

Kevin grinned. He had an idea!

'A new shipment just came in,' Kevin whispered to Ben, as they hid outside a warehouse.

Kevin crept up to the locked door. There was an electronic keypad on the wall. The keypad fizzled as Kevin held his hand over it. With a **CLUNK** the lock slid open, and the boys stepped inside. Neither saw the security alarm blink as they entered.

Wooden boxes were stacked up inside. Kevin prised one of the lids open. He tossed Ben the new Sumo Slammers game.

'Wait's over, dude,' Kevin grinned.

'Yesss!' cheered Ben, before the sound of glass shattering caught his attention. He turned round to see four metal cylinders come crashing through the windows. The canisters began to spray choking tear gas.

With a screeching of tyres and a blaring of sirens, a squad of police cars skidded to a stop outside the warehouse. Overhead, Ben could hear helicopters swooping closer. His stomach tightened into a knot as he realised that he and Kevin were completely surrounded!

CHAPTER THREE

SHOO, FLY, SHOO!

Ben coughed. The tear gas was filling the warehouse. They didn't have much time.

'What do we do?' he wheezed.

'Get outta here!' Kevin cried.

They ran. Spotting a power socket, Kevin stopped. He touched it and energy shot up his arm. The warehouse was lit by a bright blue light as Kevin drained it of power.

The warehouse doors burst open, and two policemen came running in. They both wore gas masks and each one held a powerful rifle.

'Freeze, punks!' they yelled.

Quickly, Kevin leapt into a forklift truck. His hand glowed as the truck roared into life.

'Time to rev things up!'

Kevin sent the truck forwards. It trapped the policemen against a stack of crates.

'Let's go!' Kevin cried. He and Ben ran to the exit, but a police car blocked the way.

'Great,' groaned Ben as they ducked behind a crate. 'No way out.'

'Any ideas?' asked Kevin. Ben glanced at the watch. He knew he shouldn't, but. . .

Ben twisted the dial on the Omnitrix, searching for the one alien who could get them out of this mess.

'What are you doing with your watch?' Kevin frowned.

Ben didn't answer. Instead, he slammed his hand down hard on the watch.

Energy swirled around him as Ben began to transform. He had become the alien insect, Stinkfly!

'Uh! You reek!' Kevin winced.

'I know!'

Outside, policemen edged towards the doors. Suddenly they were sent tumbling as a green shape shot past them. Helplessly, they watched it soar off across the water.

Stinkfly swooped over the waves, carrying Kevin below him. Kevin could hardly believe what was happening.

'And people call me a freak. How'd you do that?'

'Talk later,' hissed Stinkfly. He had spotted a squadron of police helicopters following close behind.

Stinkfly sped up towards the Statue of Liberty, which towered above the New York harbour. Two of the police helicopters swung round the statue's left side looking for the alien. A third had flown round on the right, but their target was nowhere to be seen.

Down below one of the helicopters, Stinkfly and Kevin clung tightly on.

'I'm running out of time,' Stinkfly warned. 'I'll try and lose them in the city.'

Stinkfly dropped down from the underside of the helicopter. Machine-gun fire followed him as he sped down towards the New York streets.

The helicopters were catching up. But Stinkfly kept low to the ground, dodging traffic. The pilots wouldn't open fire in such a crowded place.

But Stinkfly was wrong. A spray of bullets bounced off the ground close to the his head. The police were shooting to kill!

Stinkfly continued to weave through the city streets. But no matter which way he turned, the helicopters followed. And they were getting closer. This was getting really bad.

Stinkfly didn't notice The Rust Bucket, but Gwen and Grandpa noticed him – and the helicopters. They watched in horror until he flew round a corner and out of sight.

'Can't shake 'em!' Stinkfly gasped.

The three helicopters had rounded the bend behind him. He spotted a huge car transporter about to drive under a bridge below. 'I've got an idea,' he buzzed.

The pilots watched the giant insect fly down towards the transporter. It was too close to the bridge for them to get in front. They'd catch it on the other side.

When the truck drove out from under the bridge, there was no sign of the creature they had been chasing. Instead, two boys sat in one of the cars, enjoying the ride.

Ben walked along an alleyway, with Kevin at his side.

'So that watch lets you be that dragonfly thing whenever you want?' Kevin quizzed.

'And not just that one,' boasted Ben. 'I can turn into ten different aliens.'

'So the speed guy at the arcade was you?' he grinned. 'Show me what else you can morph into.'

'It's not that simple.' Ben shrugged. 'It has a mind of its own.'

'Gimme it,' Kevin demanded. 'Maybe I can make it work.'

'Can't. It's stuck on my wrist.'

'We should be partners,' Kevin said. 'We could do what we want, whenever we want.' He held his hand out to Ben. 'Friends?'

Ben hesitated, but then gave Kevin's hand a shake. 'Friends,' he said with a nod.

The Rust Bucket sped through the streets of the city.

'Of all the stunts Ben's pulled, this is the worst,' Grandpa Max growled. 'When I find him . . .'

Gwen gulped. She'd never seen her grandfather this mad before. She wouldn't like to be in Ben's shoes when they caught up with him.

'I should really be enjoying this,' she sighed. 'So why aren't I?'

Kevin and Ben hopped over a gate and onto an empty subway station platform. The lights were on, so it was still in use.

'Gimme a boost,' said Kevin. 'I need to recharge.'

Ben lifted him towards one of the lights. Once charged, Kevin hopped on to the tracks. He touched a lever, sending a bolt of energy crackling along it. A section of track rotated then locked into a new position with a **CLANK**.

'What are we doing?' asked Ben.

'A money train loaded with cash comes down this track,' explained Kevin. 'So when it crashes into the oncoming passenger train – **BOOM!** – instant jackpot! You turn into that XLR8 guy and we're outta here!'

Ben gasped. 'But hundreds of innocent people will be killed!'

Kevin's face broke into a wide grin. 'Hey,' he cackled, 'no pain, no gain!'

CHAPTER FOUR

FRIENDS NO MORE

'**Y**ou can't do this!' cried Ben.

'Sure we can,' Kevin replied.

'I just switched the tracks!'

Ben growled. 'I'm not gonna let you do this.'

'We're partners,' snarled Kevin.

'No. This is going way too far.'

'Then try and stop me, watch-boy.'

Ben remembered something Grandpa Max had said to him.

'You don't care about anyone but yourself,' Ben whispered.

'You talking about me?' demanded Kevin.

'No,' said Ben. 'I'm talking about me.'
A flash of energy struck Ben.

'You do not want to make me mad,' warned Kevin.

'Me neither,' growled Ben. 'I'm switching the track back.' He gave the Omnitrix a twist.

With a flash, Ben transformed into Heatblast.

'Move back,' Heatblast commanded.

'Or what? You're going to burn my dinner?' laughed Kevin.

'You're the one who's gonna be burned,' replied Heatblast.

Before Heatblast could do anything, Kevin sent electrical energy into the station's power grid. The overhead lights exploded, plunging the area into darkness.

Only Heatblast was visible. His glowing flames made him an easy target. He looked around for Kevin, but the boy was nowhere to be seen.

Suddenly, a pair of arms wrapped round Heatblast's neck from behind. Kevin clung on, but not for long. A burst of hot energy shot up his arm, making him cry out in pain. He dropped from the alien's back and rolled to safety.

Heatblast searched for Kevin. Something shone nearby and the alien stepped closer to take a look.

Suddenly a ball of flame knocked him over. He gasped as something that wasn't quite Kevin appeared. His head and one arm were exactly like Heatblast!

'I absorb energy, remember?' laughed Kevin.

'You don't have to do this!' said Heatblast. He threw himself at Kevin, but the boy was too fast. Kevin struck him on the back with another fireball, sending the alien crashing on to the tracks.

Heatblast was about to pull himself up when he heard a rumble in the distance. A train was coming.

He heard another sound coming from the opposite direction. Kevin had been right - the trains were going to crash!

Heatblast knew he had only one chance. He launched a jet of flame at the handle, switching the tracks. Just before the trains collided, the lever melted, switching the tracks back to their original position.

But now the money train was headed straight for Heatblast. Flames erupted from the alien before the train thundered across the spot where Heatblast had stood.

Kevin watched as the fire faded. Ben must have been finished off by the train.

But he was wrong. As the money train raced along, Heatblast clung on to the roof. But his grip slipped and the alien skidded along the train.

He managed to blast one of the carriages with a mini fireball, creating a hole. Heatblast forced his fingers inside and held on for all he was worth.

Now he had a handhold he could relax. Eventually the train would stop and he could hop off. What could possibly go wrong?

BLEEP BLEEP BLEEP BLEEEEP! The watch flashed a worrying shade of red. Realising what was about to happen, Heatblast sighed.

'Oh, man, I hate that sound!'

A few streets away, The Rust Bucket skidded round a bend.

In the passenger seat, Gwen fiddled with the short-range radio, trying to pick up emergency service broadcasts. With a crackle of static, they started to pick up a transmission.

'. . . and expect delays on the uptown subway lines near Fifty-First Street,' warned the announcer. 'There have been reports of fires breaking out all over the tunnels.'

'Grandpa!' Gwen gasped.

Grandpa Max nodded. 'I know!'

On top of the train, Ben was finding it hard to hang on. The wind's icy chill was forcing him to loosen his grip. Any moment now he was going to slip.

The honking of a horn caught his attention. The Rust Bucket was speeding along beside the train. A canopy extended from the side of the motorhome. If he could land on that, he'd be safe.

Ben took a deep breath and got ready to leap. Closing his eyes and gritting his teeth, Ben let go – and jumped!

CHAPTER FIVE

SIX ARMS ARE BETTER THAN FOUR

*B*en thudded against the canopy. He was thrown around wildly, and for a moment he thought he was going to bounce off. The Rust Bucket slowed down, and Ben got a better grip.

'None of this would have happened if you'd just obeyed me from the beginning!' snapped Grandpa Max, when Ben was back inside the motor-home. 'It's all about trust.'

'Then trust me that Kevin's probably misusing Heatblast's power right now!' replied Ben.

'OK,' sighed Grandpa Max, 'so where is he?'

Ben thought hard. What did he know about Kevin? Where would he go? What would he –? Of course!

'I think I know,' said Ben gravely. He turned the Omnitrix's dial. 'Going Stinkfly. See you at the Thirty-Ninth Street bridge!'

With a flash of energy, Ben transformed into an enormous red-skinned alien. He was so big he could barely fit in the back of The Rust Bucket.

'Great,' he muttered. 'Now I turn into Four Arms!'

A familiar gang of boys were having the worst night of their lives. They scrambled away from Kevin, trying to avoid the fireballs he hurled at them.

'We can work it out!' begged the leader.

'I don't think so,' Kevin snarled. With a blast, he brought a section of the bridge crashing on top of the gang, trapping them underneath. Kevin pointed an arm towards the trapped boys and smiled.

'So much for your gang!'

With a sudden **WHOOSH**, Kevin's Heatblast energy faded away, leaving him normal once again.

'What's going on?' he demanded.

'Your power's gone,' boomed a voice from behind him. Four Arms landed heavily on the concrete floor, cracking it into pieces.

'Looks like you're about to give me some more, Ben.'

'No.'

Kevin held his hands over the heads of the gang members. Energy crackled from his palms.

'You don't have a choice,' Kevin smirked. 'I've still got enough juice to fry these guys.'

Four Arms stepped forwards and snatched Kevin up before he could hurt anyone. But he'd walked right into his enemy's trap.

Kevin pressed his hands against the alien's arms and felt a wave of energy surge through his body as he soaked up Ben's alien power.

He threw an elbow back, smashing Four Arms in the face. When Kevin stood back up, he had transformed into a twisted version of the four-armed giant.

Kevin thundered forwards. As he ran, another pair of arms sprouted from his shoulders. He lashed out with a punch which caught Four Arms and sent him crashing into some concrete blocks.

Kevin cracked all six sets of knuckles at once. 'This is gonna be real fun!'

'Tell me about it,' Four Arms replied, getting back to his feet.

He ducked, avoiding a flurry of wild punches from Kevin. Moving fast, Four Arms caught his opponent by the wrists, and the two giants began to grapple each other.

'I'm taking all your alien powers!' Kevin growled. His two extra arms caught Four Arms by the throat and threw him against a wall. Kevin then slammed the alien's head down onto the concrete.

Up on the bridge, Grandpa Max and Gwen leaped from The Rust Bucket. There was nothing they could do to help Ben, but they could help the trapped gang.

'Moving day,' Grandpa Max told them as he cleared the rubble. 'Get out!'

The gang ran off. A mass of limbs hit the side of the bridge. Kevin and Four Arms were locked in battle.

Without warning, the Omnitrix started to flash and bleep. The transformation was about to wear off!

Four Arms gave it everything he had. Punches rained down on Kevin's head. He slammed his feet against Kevin's chest, then followed up with a shoulder-slam, sending Kevin crashing into one of the bridge's support pillars.

'C'mon, I give. I'm sorry!' Kevin wailed. 'I just went too wild with power! I don't have anyone like you to help me.'

'We can still be partners,' Ben offered, back to his human form. 'We'd just be kicking butt for good instead of bad.'

Ben stretched out his hand to Kevin in an offer of friendship. But instead of shaking his hand, Kevin grabbed Ben's wrist, lifting him high up into the air.

'Now give me the watch!' Kevin cackled, giving the Omnitrix a tug.

'I told you I can't take it off!'

Kevin gave the watch another pull. As he did, a bolt of energy surged from inside the device. The blast launched them both in opposite directions.

Ben hurtled into his grandpa's arms, while Kevin smashed through the bridge. It crumpled and collapsed on top of him.

When Kevin pulled himself free, he was back to his old self. 'Nooo!' he screamed, then fled into the city.

'I'm sorry, Grandpa,' said Ben.

Grandpa Max nodded solemnly. 'I know you are. But my trust is something you'll have to earn back.'

Ben watched Grandpa Max go. He'd prove to his grandpa that he was trustworthy, even if it took all summer.

In an abandoned subway station, a figure sat in the shadows. As a flame sprung up from his hand, Kevin laughed. It echoed before being swallowed up by the darkness.